# WEDNESDAY WILSON
## CONNECTS THE DOTS

To all the kids brimming with ideas on how to make their impact on the world, you are the inspiration for my books, so please keep dreaming! — B.G.

Text © 2023 Bree Galbraith
Illustrations © 2023 Morgan Goble

Published in Canada and the U.S. by Kids Can Press Ltd.
25 Dockside Drive, Toronto, ON  M5A 0B5

Kids Can Press is a Corus Entertainment Inc. company

www.kidscanpress.com

The artwork in this book was rendered digitally.
The text is set in Baskerville.

Edited by Katie Scott
Designed by Andrew Dupuis

Printed and bound in Shenzhen, China, in 10/2022 by C & C Offset

CM 23  0 9 8 7 6 5 4 3 2 1

**Library and Archives Canada Cataloguing in Publication**

Title: Wednesday Wilson connects the dots / written by Bree Galbraith ; illustrated by Morgan Goble.
Names: Galbraith, Bree, author. | Goble, Morgan, 1996– illustrator.
Identifiers: Canadiana 20220226164 | ISBN 9781525303296 (hardcover)
Classification: LCC PS8613.A4592 W37 2023 | DDC jC813/.6 — dc23

Kids Can Press gratefully acknowledges that the land on which our office is located is the traditional territory of many nations, including the Mississaugas of the Credit, the Anishnabeg, the Chippewa, the Haudenosaunee and the Wendat peoples, and is now home to many diverse First Nations, Inuit and Métis peoples.

We thank the Government of Ontario, through Ontario Creates; the Ontario Arts Council; the Canada Council for the Arts; and the Government of Canada for supporting our publishing activity.

# WEDNESDAY WILSON
## CONNECTS THE DOTS

Written by BREE GALBRAITH

Illustrated by MORGAN GOBLE

KIDS CAN PRESS

# CONTENTS

# CHAPTER 1
## Early Riser

My favorite kind of school day is one like today, when I don't have to go to school at all. Over the weekend, a pipe at school burst, so even though it's Monday, the school is closed while they clean up all the water. I know what you're thinking: What about Morten, our class lizard? But don't worry — Ms. Gelson takes Morten home on the weekends, so he's safe.

It might be Monday, but it feels like the weekend because Charlie slept over. I'm not ever allowed sleepovers on school nights, but Charlie's mom went on a date last night, so my moms made a "special exception" to their rule. They said it was because it's not technically a school night, plus Charlie's sister is away at a water polo tournament and it's not his dad's weekend to be with them. But I think it's because they were excited for Charlie's mom.

As much as Charlie loves sleeping over, he said he'd trade all the sleepovers in the world if it meant his mom wouldn't go on a date. He doesn't want to share his mom with anyone else. To take his mind off it, we watched *Eagle Eye* and then brainstormed our own business ideas until we fell asleep.

Even though it's still dark outside, I'm too excited to go back to sleep — and not just because I don't have to go to school today. I'm waiting for my mum to let me know it's time to get the Teresaria ready for the day. She's always up before dawn to set up her pizza truck, and she said today I can help. She doesn't know it yet, but I slept in my clothes so I could get ready even faster.

"Wednesday?" my mum whispers through the door.

I quietly jump out of bed and hop over Charlie's mattress on the floor. "Ready!" I tell her, opening the door to my room.

"Shhh!" she says. "Let's go!"

Maybe I wasn't as quiet as I thought.

We tiptoe downstairs and get all the tubs of toppings out of our fridge. Then we head out to the driveway, where the Teresaria is parked. I like it when it's just me and my mum in the early morning. It makes me feel like we're the only two entrepreneurs awake this early, and putting in this kind of effort is what it takes to make it big.

I know I just said I'm an entrepreneur, but the truth is that I haven't had a ton of luck in business yet. One of the investors on *Eagle Eye* said that half of small businesses fail within the first few years, so it's not like it's easy or anything. Especially not for an eight-year-old. But I'm not giving up.

My first job this morning is to fill my mum's pizza-making station with all the ingredients while she writes the weekly special on the menu. Last night, we had a competition to invent a new pizza for the special, and for dinner we taste-tested them all. I wanted to order sushi instead, but my moms said no.

# LAST NIGHT'S PIZZA INVENTIONS

sushi pizza
(Wednesday)

peanut butter and
banana pizza (Mister)

spicy cauliflower pizza
(Mum)

fungi feast pizza
(Mom)

macaroni and cheese pizza
(Charlie)

Charlie's pizza won the taste test, and so Mum adds the Charlino to her sign.

My next task is counting the money in the cash register so my mum knows what she'll be starting the day with. I could count money all day.

"Are you sure you don't want me and Charlie to come with you?" I ask. Maybe this will be the day she says yes!

"Of course I *want* you to come," my mum tells me. "But I think your time is better spent working on your own business today."

I agree with her, and not just because she's the kind of parent who doesn't change her mind. I let her know that Charlie and I could use the day to work on the businesses we came up with last night.

"Maybe you could run some of your ideas by me before I take off?" says my mum as she does one last wipe of the countertops.

I share the ideas Charlie and I brainstormed that were inspired by the burst pipe that gave us the day off.

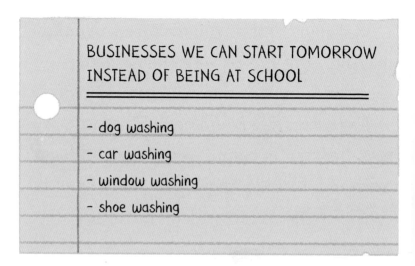

BUSINESSES WE CAN START TOMORROW
INSTEAD OF BEING AT SCHOOL

- dog washing
- car washing
- window washing
- shoe washing

My mum laughs. "That sure is a lot of washing for someone who doesn't like to clean," she says. "Can I give you a bit of advice? You can think of me as a business consultant*."

*A business consultant is someone who gives you advice on how to run your business. They can help you make more money or treat your employees better, which Mister says are things I need to work on.

I nod.

"If I didn't love making pizza and seeing people smile after taking that first bite, I couldn't imagine getting up this early to get the Teresaria ready for the day," she says.

Then she points to a framed quote on the wall of her food truck.

"If you do work that you love, and the work fulfills you, the rest will come."
— Oprah

Oprah's right. I need my business to be about something that I love doing. And

Mum's right, too — I do not like to clean. Charlie and I have some rethinking to do.

I say goodbye and head back inside. That's when I hear Mom on the phone in the kitchen, and I get the sense that Charlie and I won't have much time for rethinking because this day has a plan of its own.

"Ruby is always welcome to come over!" she tells the person on the other end of the line. "See you soon!"

## CHAPTER 2
# Facon Till You Make It

While I wait for Ruby to get here, I worry about what we're going to talk about all day. She hasn't said more than three words to me and Charlie since last summer, after she went to a birthday sleepover for Emma Meng, the meanest of the Emmas. Before that, me, Charlie and Ruby were best friends since forever. But after the sleepover, she was suddenly best friends with the Emmas, who then started calling her Ruby Beautiful.

I know you're thinking I'm leaving out something important, like the reason why Ruby stopped talking to us, but trust me, I'm not. You know as much as I do, which means you also know how awkward it's going to be when she comes over.

My mom sees the look on my face as soon as she puts the phone down.

"Ruby's mom has to go to work," she tells me before I can say anything, "and her dad just got called for an important job interview."

I roll my eyes and sigh. "Can't Raj look after her?" I don't usually roll my eyes around my moms, but this situation calls for it.

"Wednesday Wilson!" my mom scolds. "Like I told her dad on the phone, Ruby is always welcome here. Can you please make the best of it? For me?"

I don't say anything else because I don't want to get in trouble. But I wish Mom understood how hard it is to make the best out of the worst day possible. Worse than having a math test. Worse than having homework. And double worse than having to go to school in the first place.

Before I can argue, Mister rushes downstairs, still in his pajamas. "Can I make facon pancakes?" he asks Mom. She agrees and lets Mister take charge of breakfast.

"Good morning," says Charlie, following close behind. "What's facon?"

"Fake bacon. Don't worry. It will taste good with syrup," I reassure him.

Charlie and I sit at the kitchen island as Mister pulls out all the ingredients from the fridge and cupboards. He and my mom make the best pancakes. They say cooking is like art — and that's how we end up eating things like facon pancakes.

I place my clipboard down in front of me and Charlie. Now would be a good time to tell him that Ruby is on her way over, but there's no point in us both being stressed out before she even gets here. Instead, I say, "I think we have work to do."

I explain the conversation I had earlier with my mum.

Charlie admits that he wasn't that excited about any of the businesses on our list, since he's not so good at washing things anyway.

"Whatever we do, we'll have to fake it till we make it," I say confidently. "We aren't experts at anything yet, Charlie, but it doesn't mean we won't be."

Charlie likes the sound of this. He says he'd rather invent a shoe-cleaning robot than scrub people's dirty shoes. I start to add that to our new list of business ideas when Mister interrupts.

"Ruby's watching," Mister says.

"I'm not sure Ruby-watching would make us any money," Charlie replies. "Plus, she and the Emmas are already the best spies at school."

"No," says Mister. "Ruby *is* watching." He points to the window beside the front door, where we see Ruby and her brother, Raj, about to ring the doorbell.

"I meant to tell you …" I whisper to Charlie. But it's too late.

Charlie erupts with one of his facts, which happens whenever he's stressed out. "The flapjack octopus flattens down like a pancake to appear less threatening to its prey!"

Speaking of prey, why do I feel like we're about to be eaten alive?

# CHAPTER 3
## Time to Makeup

"Good morning, you two!" says my mom as she invites Ruby and Raj inside.

Raj has to give Ruby a little push to get her to step into our house. She keeps her head down the whole time and avoids eye contact with me and Charlie.

"Good morning, Mrs. Wilson," says Raj. "Thank you so much for looking after Ruby today. We're very thankful, right, Rubes?"

"Yes, thank you, Mrs. Wilson," says Ruby quietly.

"No problem!" says my mom. "She can help Wednesday and Charlie with their start-up*!"

Ruby puts down her backpack and hovers around her brother at the door. I'm not sure what's more uncomfortable, me trying to avoid eye contact with Ruby or glancing to see if she's avoiding eye contact with me.

"I'd watch Ruby myself, but I have an exam to study for," Raj explains.

"What's your exam on?" my mom asks. Raj is training to be a makeup artist,

*A start-up is a brand-new company that's still very young — before it becomes a fully grown business. Whenever people tell me that I'm too young to start a business, I just say that most start-ups also have a lot of growing up to do.

and since my mom is an artist, they can talk for hours about this stuff.

"I'm learning about semi-permanent makeup," Raj explains. "It's like tattooing makeup on your face — eyebrows, lipstick, even freckles — that eventually wears off. Everybody wants it these days."

"Coolio!" my mom says. "I'll look out for your next video."

Raj has a bajillion followers on social media who watch his makeup tutorials. I silently cringe at the thought of my mom commenting something like "coolio" on one of his videos and Ruby seeing it. Thankfully, Raj is in a hurry and has to leave, so my mom doesn't have the chance to say anything else embarrassing.

A few minutes later, Ruby sits down at the kitchen table and pretends to read the book she brought. My mom explains she has a call with her art agent and a potential client. Before she heads to her studio, she kisses me on the head and whispers, "Remember — make the best of it." So much for not doing anything else embarrassing.

Mister grabs the platter of pancakes, and the three of us join Ruby at the table. I pass out plates to everyone. Even Ruby. No one says a word. I think we could set the record for the quietest eating of facon pancakes in the world.

When I glance over at Charlie, he's looking nervously into his lap, and his eye is twitching. I just know he's about to cut the tension with another fact, and I want to save him from being a funny story that Ruby will tell the Emmas at school tomorrow.

"Dog walking!" I exclaim.

"What?" ask Mister and Charlie together.

"Dog walking," I repeat. "That's our next business! I love dogs. Dogs love me."

"Where do we find dogs to walk?" Ruby asks excitedly. We all turn to look at her. "I mean you. Not we. Obviously. Or whatever." Then she quickly looks back at her book.

"Easy!" I say. "The off-leash dog park!" Not only is the dog park just down the street, but it has all the customers we'll ever need.

"We should make signs," says Charlie, "to advertise our dog-walking business."

"Good idea!" I reply. "Mister, grab some pens and paper. I'll grab tape."

Mister gets the supplies and has an idea right away. A moment later, he proudly holds up our first sign.

"We can put them on poles so they're easy to read when dogs go for a walk," Mister says.

"Dogs can't read," I tell him.

"You don't know that for sure," Mister replies. "But what I meant is that their owners can read the signs while the dogs do their business."

Ruby tries to hide her laugh. "Just don't put them too low or they might get peed on. I'm not sure that's the kind of business you're looking for."

We all burst out laughing. It feels almost like it used to with Ruby, like she's back to her old self again — the one who told me I was going to be the most successful entrepreneur in the world one day. When she's not noticing, I glance at Ruby to see if her old self is still in there.

# CHAPTER 4
## Choosing Sides

I run to my mom's studio to let her know we're going to the dog park. My mom tells me we have to stay together, to be back for lunch and that no dogs are allowed to come home with me.

When we arrive at the dog park, we scout for potential clients in the giant fenced-in area. The dog owners from our neighborhood are watching their dogs run around, and all I can see are dollar signs. Some are small and fluffy dollar signs, and some are big and slobbery dollar signs, and they all start to add up.

I haven't told anyone yet, but I have a
secret ingredient that will attract every
dog in the park. I bring out the handful of
facon bits from my pocket, and suddenly, a
white poodle covered in poofy pom-poms
appears at my side. It's wearing a pink
collar and two shiny pink bows on each
ear that look oddly familiar.

"Douglas?" cries Ruby when she sees the dog.

"Ruby Beautiful?!" comes a voice from behind us. "There you are!"

It's Emma M., and she's got the other two Emmas with her. They're all wearing matching heart sweaters and have shiny pink bows in their hair. And they think *I'm* weird!

"Emma M.? Emma A.? Emma N.?" Ruby stammers. "What are you doing here?"

"Duh, we're helping Emma M. walk Douglas," say Emma A. and Emma N. in unison as they point to the poodle. I wonder if Emma M. is mind-controlling them.

"And we're obviously coordinating our look for picture day tomorrow," adds Emma N. "We told you on Friday that was the plan."

"The real question," Emma M. asks me, "is why are you playing with bacon?"

All of the Emmas burst out laughing.

"It's facon," Mister replies, which only makes them laugh more.

"And we're not playing with it," says Charlie, turning red. "We're looking for dogs."

"Whatever. We're here to rescue you, Ruby," says Emma M.

Ruby looks like she'd rather be anywhere in the world but here, but she doesn't move.

"Ruby!" says Emma M. "Let's go!"

"I can't," says Ruby. "My parents said … I mean … I have to —"

"Look for dogs?" Emma A. interrupts. "Seriously?" She rolls her eyes much better than I did this morning.

"I have to stay with Wednesday today," says Ruby. There's an irritated tone in her voice, and I wonder if she finally understands how it feels to be teased by the Emmas.

"Don't tell me this is one of Wednesday's business things," says Emma N. Then all three of the Emmas erupt in more laughter.

"So what if it is?!" I demand. "Why do you even care?"

"We don't," says Emma M., stroking her hair. "But FYI, if you're looking for dogs, there's one over there that looks just like Charlie. It's got funny spots all over it."

The Emmas laugh, and Charlie looks like he might cry. I feel like this is all my fault for bringing us to the dog park in the first place.

"They're not funny spots. They're freckles!" I say. Then I think of what my mom would say. She's always telling me that people are meanest when they're insecure. "You're just jealous because you don't have any."

Emma M. steps up to me. "People don't *want* freckles, Wednesday," she says. "They're just born with them."

"That's not true!" I reply. I can feel myself growing angrier by the second.

"Says who?" Emma M. demands.

"SAYS RAJ!" yells Ruby, who now seems super annoyed. We all go completely silent.

Ruby takes a deep breath and steps between me and Emma M. "Raj said that people pay tons of money to get freckles tattooed on their faces."

"*Raj* said that?" the Emmas say in unison. I can see their eyes light up with interest.

The Emmas aren't just in love with Raj, they are obsessed with him. They even started the Raj Bajwa Fan Club last year after he reached half a million followers on social media.

"Yes, he did," Ruby continues. "He also said that his freckle tutorial video got two million views. So Wednesday is right."

That's when I realize that dog walking isn't the business we need to start today.

"THAT'S IT!" I yell. I throw my hands in the air, forgetting about the facon, and Douglas inhales the crumbs after they fall from the sky.

## CHAPTER 5
## Get Your Freckle On

Everyone turns to me.

I look at the Emmas and tell them with confidence, "We're not actually looking for dogs — we're advertising our freckle service. And we only have time for paying customers, so goodbye!"

Emma M. clicks a pink leash to Douglas's pink collar. "You're the one who should leave, Wednesday. You don't even have a dog. And I doubt you even have a business."

"We do so. As a matter of fact, we are just about to put up our first sign." I turn my back to the Emmas and pull Charlie and Mister into a huddle. "Quick! We need a name for our business!"

"What is our business again?" asks Charlie. Ruby edges closer to us.

"Freckles!" I say too loudly. "We're going to give people freckles with some of my mom's fancy markers," I explain.

Mister and Charlie aren't convinced, but they do seem interested. The Emmas are on the opposite side of Ruby, and they are busy whispering, too.

"You mean you were serious?" asks Charlie. "A freckle service?"

"You heard Ruby," I tell him, pulling Ruby into the circle. "People pay money for freckles, right, Ruby? So why not pay us for them?"

"I thought you guys were just standing up for me," says Charlie.

"I was standing up for you," Ruby whispers. "But it's also true that Raj told me how popular his freckle video was."

I ask again for some names for our new business. You know when you think too hard about something, and then you end up not having any ideas? That's what is happening with me.

"How about Five-Cent Freckles?" says Mister.

"I like it, but I think we should charge ten cents per freckle," I say. Everyone agrees.

"Freckles-R-Us?" suggests Charlie.

We share a few more ideas, but none of them have a good enough ring to them. *Think, Wednesday. THINK!* I say to myself.

"Frecktacular!" Ruby whispers.

It's perfect! Mister writes it on our new sign.

I tape the sign to the dog park fence, right in front of Emma M. The Emmas stop whispering, and I brace myself for how they'll make fun of our new business.

Instead, Emma M. ignores the sign and makes one last attempt to "rescue" Ruby. "Come on, *Rubes*," she says, using the nickname I've only ever heard Raj use. "My dad's ordering sushi for lunch, so you don't have to eat Wednesday's gross pocket facon."

"I can't hang out today, Emma," Ruby says. "I'm staying with Wednesday."

The Emmas narrow their eyes at me like I purposely ruined their day.

"You'll pay for this, Wednesday," Emma M. says under her breath as the Emmas walk past us. She leads Douglas, with his poofy pom-poms, out of the off-leash area.

"Let's forget about them," says Charlie when we're safely out of earshot.

We all agree. Even Ruby. She's the one who suggests we make a list of things we need to do to get started with Frecktacular. I pull out my clipboard.

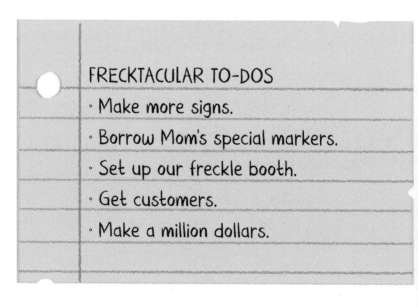

FRECKTACULAR TO-DOS
- Make more signs.
- Borrow Mom's special markers.
- Set up our freckle booth.
- Get customers.
- Make a million dollars.

I volunteer to go home to get Mom's special markers, the ones with the super-small tips that will be perfect for making freckles. Plus, it's almost lunchtime, and I can ask Mom if I can bring back food for everyone. I leave my clipboard with Mister and delegate* the sign-making to him while I'm gone.

"Do you think we will get in trouble for setting up a business in the park?" asks Charlie.

"It's technically not the school park, so I don't think Principal Webb can get mad

*Delegating is an important business skill, and it means asking someone to do something that you could do yourself to spread the work around. Mister says I'm a little too good at delegating, like when I ask him to clean my room for me.

at us this time," I answer. "Plus, she can't make the rules on our day off!"

"You got in trouble with Principal Webb?" Ruby asks.

I realize there's so much she's missed out on, good and not-so-good. We have a lot of catching up to do.

As I run home, I feel both excited and nervous that Ruby chose us over the Emmas. I'm excited that I might have my old friend back, but nervous about what the Emmas said about making me pay. But then I laugh out loud. I mean, what could they possibly do?

# CHAPTER 6
## Paid in Full

"Mom!" I call when I get back home. "Mom?" I can't find her in the living room or in the kitchen. "MOMMMMMM!" I yell as I enter her art studio. The familiar smell of paint greets me right away.

"I'm taking a moment to recharge," she tells me from her yoga mat on the floor, where she's sitting with her eyes closed.

She's surrounded by cans upon cans of paint. In the middle of the room is a giant colorful sketch of the mural she's working on for a taco restaurant downtown. Being in Mom's studio feels like walking inside a kaleidoscope.

As I get closer, my mom opens her eyes. She looks like she's been crying.

"I came back to get lunch for everyone," I explain. "Are you okay?"

"Yes, my love," she says, standing up. "Just trying not to let some disappointment get the best of me. You know that mural I've been working on?"

I nod.

"Well, I decided it's not going to work out," she replies.

"Why not?" I ask her. I was looking forward to telling my friends all about it. It's the coolest taco place in the city. I try to hide my disappointment at missing out on all those free tacos.

"They didn't want to pay me what I'm worth," she tells me. "And if you undervalue yourself, you set a standard for other people to do the same thing."

Until this very second, I hadn't seen my mom as someone who runs a business. But now I understand that her art is her business! Maybe I'm a lot like both my moms.

"When I'm rich, I'll buy your art at full price," I tell her. "No matter what."

"Thank you, Wednesday," she replies. Then she gives me a hug.

I also understand why she's so upset, because I heard her and Mum talking the other night about how they needed that mural job to pay the bills. Maybe your parents have the same conversations about money, too? I don't know about you, but I get nervous whenever I overhear my parents talk about this stuff. It's another reason I want to be rich — so neither of my moms need to worry about not having enough money for things.

We head into the kitchen to gather up whatever we can for lunch, which means as many boxes of leftover pizza as I can carry in Mister's wagon. I don't want to upset

Mom any further, so I don't tell her I'd
rather eat literally anything else for lunch.
Instead, I just pile the boxes into the wagon.
There's three cheese, facon-potato and kale.
I don't even want to think about the kale
pizza, so I shove it to the bottom of the pile.
Suddenly, a flavor comes to mind — taco!

"Mum should make a taco pizza and
steal all their customers!" I tell her.

"I'm not into the *stealing* part," she says,
smiling, "but there's nothing wrong with
some healthy competition!"

My mom's phone rings. The screen says
"TACO."

"Maybe it's good news!" I tell her.

"One can hope," she replies. Mom
takes a deep breath in and lets it out before

answering. She heads into the small office my moms share for their work stuff and blows me a kiss goodbye.

I'm halfway out the door when I remember the most important thing — the markers! Mister and I aren't exactly supposed to use Mom's expensive art supplies, but I don't have a chance to ask her permission to borrow them since she's still on the phone. I grab her plastic case of markers from her studio and hide them under the pizza boxes in the wagon.

As I roll the wagon down my street to the dog park, my stomach grumbles at the thought of a taco pizza. And then my stomach suddenly drops. There's a sign advertising a freckle service, but it doesn't look like Mister's artwork. It's been made on a computer, and the price per freckle is only five cents — half of what we agreed on. Did my friends decide to change things without me?

I tear the sign off the pole and follow five more signs back to the picnic table that Mister, Charlie and Ruby have claimed for our booth.

"Wednesday," says Ruby, "we have a problem."

I see that everyone on my team has one of the weird signs in their hands.

Ruby points behind me, where the Emmas have set up their own freckle booth right across the street. "That's how they're going to make you pay."

# CHAPTER 7
# Healthy Competition

I turn my back to the Emmas' freckle booth, and my mind starts racing.

*Why are they copying us now when they usually make fun of our businesses?*

*Why set up shop directly across the street?*

*Why does Douglas have a sign on his back?*

A friendly voice interrupts my thoughts.

"Wednesday!" calls Amina, running over to us. "My daycare leader let us all follow your signs here. This is so cool!"

I'm glad Amina thinks a freckle service is a cool idea, but I explain to her that it wasn't our signs she was following.

"We might as well give up!" says Ruby.

"Their freckles are half the price of ours," says Charlie.

"And their signs look professional," says Mister.

"And they're all dressed the same," adds Amina. "Does anyone else think that's strange?"

Today was supposed to be the day I start a new business, and not even the Emmas can stop me. If this has any chance of working, I need to keep everyone's spirits up, but it's not going to be easy.

"I'm going to talk to them," I say a little more bravely than I feel.

"Better you than me," says Charlie. His eye twitches slightly, and his cheeks start turning red. "I'd rather close up shop than go over there."

"In the meantime, can you put up our signs so they're right above the Emmas' signs?" I ask my friends. At least that way, ours seem slightly more important.

"Good idea," says Ruby.

"And good luck," whispers Amina.

*I can do this. I can do this*, I tell myself as I walk over to the Emmas. After all, Frecktacular was my idea, not theirs.

Even though their freckle booth is right across the street, it feels like it takes me an hour to get there. As I get closer, I see that their booth is just a cardboard box with a tablecloth covering it. They're each sitting on a folding chair, and there's an empty chair for customers. They have a mirror, too, which I silently wish I had thought of myself. Douglas wags his tail at me and sniffs at my pockets as I approach.

Emma M. is the first to speak. "We only have time for paying customers, Wednesday," she sneers.

"This was my idea, Emma," I tell her. "You can't do this."

"You don't own freckles," Emma N. pipes in.

I clench my teeth and take a deep breath in. "You're just doing this to cause trouble," I tell them with frustration. "You don't even like freckles! You were *just* making fun of Charlie for having them."

"Not true!" says Emma N. "Emma A. has freckles."

"Show her!" Emma M. demands.

Emma A. rolls up her sleeve and points to a brown dot on her arm. "See!" she says.

"That's a mole," I tell her. "And either way, this was still my idea."

Emma A. starts fake crying because I called her freckle a mole.

"Now look what you've done,
Wednesday," accuses Emma M. Then
she turns to Emma A. and hands her a
makeup bag with a knowing nod. "Why
don't you go to the park bathroom to
freshen up?"

As Emma A. walks off, she passes Ruby, Charlie, Amina and Mister, who are coming toward us.

"We're done with the signs," says Ruby. "Is everything okay over here?"

"I was just leaving," I tell Ruby. It feels easier to walk away with Ruby by my side.

"Whatever!" shouts Emma M. behind us. "May the best freckle booth win!"

Back at our station, I tell everyone what happened. "They're not going to shut down their booth. But there's nothing wrong with a little healthy competition."

I remember last week's episode of *Eagle Eye* where a businesswoman told the Eagles all the ways her product was better than her competitors'.* She walked away with a $100 000 investment in her business, so what she said must have worked.

I explain that we'll just have to try harder to stand out. "We have to think of all the ways that we're better than them — things that make us different, things that make us worth it."

*A competitor is like your rival in business. It's another company that is trying to get the same customers as you (a.k.a. the Emmas).

Everyone stops and thinks.

Ruby is first to share her thoughts. "Our signs are way more fun than theirs," she says.

"And our frecklers are much nicer," adds Mister.

"And we were the original freckle service, too," says Charlie. "That has to count for something, right?"

We decide that we just need to do something about our higher price, since we don't have time to redo all the signs.

"How about donating half of the money to charity?" asks Amina. "That way, both your freckles are the same price, but people who choose Frecktacular are also donating to a good cause."

"Good idea!" I tell her. I'm so glad she stopped by to visit us.

We all agree. We use our last four pieces of paper to make new signs advertising our charity, the food bank. Amina and I go to put up the rest of the signs while the others set up the booth. Then we wait to see if our plan will work.

## CHAPTER 8
## Almost Famous

When I look over at the Emmas' freckle booth, they already have a customer. Then again, it's Emma A.'s little brother, who I'm pretty sure is not paying them, so he doesn't count. I want to be the first one with a real customer. I need to do something to get people's attention.

Amina has brought over her daycare group, and they seem interested. Now is my time to turn them into paying customers.

"If you've ever dreamed of having freckles, but weren't lucky enough to be born with them, today is your day!" I tell them.

More people from the park start to gather. My next step is explaining the way it works. I try to share how each freckle is skillfully applied with one of our special markers, but my voice is no match for the expertly trained Douglas, who Emma M. has conveniently commanded to bark through my speech.

"Arooooooooooooooooo!" howls Douglas from across the street each time I say a word. "Aroooooo! Aroooooo!"

Emma M. snaps her fingers, and Douglas goes silent. "Come experience the only freckle service Douglas the Show Poodle trusts!"

Douglas howls again. He stands on his hind legs and shimmies around in a circle. He's doing a great job of getting attention. Our crowd slowly starts moving closer to the Emmas to see what their booth is all about.

A feeling of embarrassment is creeping in — I'm losing not only to the Emmas, but to a poodle, too! I sit down on the picnic table and want to cry. Real cry, not Emma cry. Ruby is the first to notice. She steps in front of me and puts her pointer finger and thumb in her

mouth, then lets out the loudest whistle I've ever heard. I'm pretty sure the whole park heard her. Even Douglas stops his performance mid-twirl.

"Gather 'round for a live demonstration!" Ruby yells, and the crowd moves back over to our booth.

"What are you doing?" I ask her.

"Just go with it," she says. "Trust me."

I'm not sure I can fully trust Ruby yet, but I want to. I try to smile as she applies freckles to my face.

She stops at fifty-two freckles and asks Amina if she can borrow her phone. Ruby snaps a picture of me and starts typing into the phone. A few seconds later, I hear the *ding* of a text message reply.

"Frecktacular has an endorsement*
from internet sensation Raj Bajwa!"
Ruby holds up the phone to the crowd
to show that Raj has just given a
thumbs-up to the photo.

I open my eyes to see that a long line
has formed behind Ruby.

"Me next!" says a fifth grader from
our school.

"And then me!" says his friend.

"Those other freckles from across the
street look like moles!" I hear someone
say.

---

*An endorsement is when someone (usually a famous
person or an expert) says that they approve of
something. It's a way to build trust in your brand, which
is something I'm learning a lot about from Ruby today.

Freshly freckled and feeling inspired, I take to the park and tell anyone who will listen. "Everyone is getting freckled over at the other end of the park! Look for the crowd! It's even been endorsed by Raj Bajwa himself! Half of all proceeds donated to the food bank!"

I'm not exaggerating when I say that a few minutes later, the line for Frecktacular wraps around the small park. Each of us takes on a role in the business perfectly suited to our talent. I walk around drumming up customers, Ruby and Mister apply freckles, and Charlie takes the money. It feels amazing to officially be in business, but I feel even better when I look across the street. The Emmas are closing up their booth!

When we finish with our last customer, Ruby and I slump on top of the table, exhausted. My voice is almost gone, and Ruby says her hand hurts from holding the marker for so long. But still, I somehow feel like it's the most fun we've both had in a long time.

While Charlie counts the money, Ruby regains just enough strength to apply freckles to Mister's face, and then Mister does the same for her. I hand out the pizza, which we were too busy to eat earlier. No one even touches the kale pizza.

"We officially put thirty-two hundred freckles on people's faces today," says Charlie. "That's three hundred and twenty dollars!"

"One hundred and sixty dollars in donations!" Ruby exclaims.

"And forty dollars each!" says Charlie. He gives everyone their share.

While we clean up, I ask everyone what they want to do with their money. I already know mine will go to my puppy fund.

"We should also pay your mom back for her markers," says Charlie. "We used some of them up." He hands me a pouch.

"What's this?" I ask him.

"Your mom's marker pouch," he replies.

"Um, it's definitely not my mom's," I tell him. I rummage through the wagon, and hidden under the kale pizza box is the plastic case with my mom's markers. I hold it up to show him.

"We were supposed to use these ones," I say, confused.

"I just grabbed the pencil case that was on top of the pizza boxes," Ruby explains.

"And I just used what Ruby was using!" says Mister.

I think back to when I arrived at the park and realize that I never took out Mom's markers from under the pizza boxes.

Charlie interrupts my thoughts. "If we weren't using your mom's markers, then whose markers are these?"

Ruby looks through the markers in the pouch, and I can see something catch her eye. She holds one up to inspect it.

We all lean in to see what she's looking at.

"Uh-oh," she says. "I think I know who these belong to, and you're not gonna be happy about it."

# CHAPTER 9
# One Mystery Solved

"Ew! They belong to the Emmas?" Mister shrieks. "Do you think they're poisonous?" He raises his hands to his newly freckled cheeks.

"No way," says Ruby immediately. "That's too far, even for the Emmas."

I agree that the Emmas would never go that far, but I'm annoyed that Ruby is sticking up for them after today. We pack up our booth, and on the way home, we try to figure out how the Emmas' markers ended up in our hands. I go over everything that happened when I was talking to the Emmas. Something doesn't feel right.

"It must have been when Emma A. went to the bathroom with the makeup pouch," I say. "But Ruby, how come you didn't know that the pouch belonged to the Emmas, since you hang out all the time?"

Ruby looks hurt. "Their pouch is usually filled with makeup, and this one had markers. I'm sorry — I honestly didn't know!"

I can tell she means it, and being mad at Ruby won't help us get to the bottom of this. But I know I'm still not totally over how she ditched me and Charlie for the Emmas last summer.

"Why did you stop being friends with us?" I suddenly blurt out. The words come out so fast it takes me a second to realize the can of worms I just opened.

"I could ask you the same thing," Ruby answers immediately.

"What are you talking about?" I reply. "Me, you and Charlie were best friends. And then BAM! You were an Emma."

"A Ruby Beautiful, to be precise," adds Charlie.

Ruby looks to us, confused. "Emma M. invited me to her birthday sleepover last summer because she said she heard I didn't have any friends. She said you and Charlie were telling people we weren't friends anymore so you wouldn't have to split your profits with me."

"She said WHAT?" I'm so shocked that I stop dead in my tracks. Starting a business has never been only about money. In fact, I've hardly made any money yet. Plus, I'd rather split whatever we make a hundred ways and do it with my friends than keep it all to myself and be without them.

Ruby continues. "So I went to the sleepover, and then they started calling me Ruby Beautiful and made me feel like I was a part of their group. And you and Charlie stopped talking to me, so I figured it was all true."

Now I add defensive to the list of things I'm feeling. "We stopped talking to you *after* you became an Emma!" I explain. "I never said that about not wanting to share the business with you! Why didn't you talk to me?"

"I guess it was easier to avoid the truth. I didn't want to know why I wasn't good enough for you," Ruby explains.

I feel angry — but not at Ruby anymore. I'm angry at the Emmas and at myself for never talking to Ruby about what was going on.

"Ruby, you have always been more than good enough," I promise her.

Ruby lets out a huge sigh. "All this time I thought you hated me," she tells us.

"Don't worry, Ruby, we're not allowed to hate anybody," says Mister. "It's one of our moms' rules."

We all laugh.

I stand on one side of Ruby, and Charlie takes the other. We start walking home again, together.

# CHAPTER 10
# Washing Up

As soon as we get back to my house, the Teresaria pulls into the driveway. Only you wouldn't recognize it because the truck is covered in bird poop. It looks like an art project gone terribly wrong.

My mom laughs from the front porch. "I guess pigeons don't like pizza?"

"I parked under the bridge for the lunch rush — and apparently right under where every pigeon in town was roosting." My mum groans. "I need to hose her down, or no one will be buying my pizza for dinner tonight!"

My mom comes back out with rubber gloves, buckets, dish soap and rags. Then my mum grabs the hose. She lets Mister pour the soap into a bucket as she fills it up with water, but he adds way too much, and soon there are so many bubbles it's hard to see one step in front of you. We all get to work scrubbing the truck, even Charlie and Ruby.

"All right, everyone, stand back!" calls my mum from beneath the bubbles. We all run for safety as she rinses the truck. The soapy foam streams off and leaves behind a sparkling shine on the Teresaria.

"You're next!" she says. Then she turns the hose toward me and Mister, Charlie and Ruby. We scream and laugh as she sprays us down. Maybe my mum was wrong this morning — maybe I do like washing things if it's this fun!

Charlie and Ruby head home soon after, leaving behind a trail of puddles. Our houses are so close I can see Ruby's dad smiling in their front window and, a few doors down, Charlie's mom laughing on their front stoop. My mum waves goodbye to them from the Teresaria as she drives down the street and back to work, poop-free.

My mom hands me and Mister towels at the door. "What's that on your faces?" she asks.

"Freckles!" Mister exclaims.

"Hmm," she replies, taking a closer look. "Where did they come from?"

"From Frecktacular," he tells her. "It's Wednesday's new idea!" Mister ditches his towel and all his wet clothes, and runs upstairs to change.

"We made forty dollars each," I tell my mom proudly.

"What did you use for these freckles, Wednesday?" she asks suspiciously. She takes the corner of the towel and scrubs at my cheek.

"We raised one hundred and sixty dollars for the food bank," I tell her.

"Nice try, but that did not answer my question," my mom says.

"We sort of borrowed your special markers, but we didn't even use them!" I say a little too quickly. "It's a long story.

But it was all because we were sticking up for Charlie. And the best part is that Ruby stuck up for him, too, and now I don't even think she's friends with the Emmas anymore!"

My mom licks her thumb and rubs my other cheek. "I hope your 'long story' can explain why these freckles are still on your face after you basically just went through a car wash."

I bring the Emmas' marker pouch to my mom, and she examines one of the markers closely. She peels off the heart stickers one by one to reveal the one word they had covered up: PERMANENT.

"On the bright side, people got their money's worth," I say with a half-smile.

My mom doesn't look convinced. "Hopefully everyone's parents look on that bright side when they get their kids' school pictures back."

Shoot! I completely forgot that tomorrow is picture day.

# CHAPTER 11
## Picture Perfect?

I wake up in the morning feeling uneasy. Mister and I went to bed with our faces full of freckles, even after our moms tried everything to get them off. Could the freckles have disappeared overnight? Half of my brain hopes they stayed because I like them, but the other half wonders if people's parents might be a teensy-weensy bit mad the freckles didn't wash off for picture day. Or a lot mad.

I get out of bed to check my face in the mirror. Still as freckly as yesterday.

When it's time to go to school, Mister and I meet Charlie and Ruby outside our house. Obviously Charlie's freckles are still there since they're the real thing, but Ruby's are, too.

"We're Frecktacular quadruplets!" says Mister.

"It's way better than matching heart sweaters, don't you think?" Ruby jokes.

Charlie laughs. "And I don't have enough hair to tie in a bow."

I'm glad my friends can laugh about it. Maybe everyone else at school will, too?

Since saying what was on my mind worked out yesterday, I ask the question that's been on the tip of my tongue after learning about what really happened with Ruby last summer. "Why do you think the Emmas made up that stuff?" I ask. "Why didn't they want us to be friends?"

"I have a feeling I know why," Ruby tells us. She shares that at Emma M.'s birthday sleepover, all the Emmas wanted to do was ask about Raj, watch his makeup tutorials and gush about how he makes people so beautiful. "They are Raj obsessed! He might be a big deal to some people, but he's just a boring brother to me. No offense, Mister."

"That's okay," says Mister. "I know what you mean."

"That's why they started calling me Ruby Beautiful, because of Raj," Ruby explains.

It sounds to me like the Emmas didn't try to get to know Ruby — they just wanted to get closer to Raj.

We hear the first bell and run the rest of the way to school. It's just like old times. When we get to the school grounds, we meet Emmet and Amina, then say goodbye to Mister as he heads toward the kindergarten entrance.

"Unfair!" says Emmet when he sees we all have freckles. He was at his grandpa's house yesterday and missed out. "I want some, too!"

As I look around, tons of freckled students from the park yesterday smile at us and say hello. The only mean looks are coming from the Emmas, and I'm used to that.

Principal Webb is at her usual place at the main door, welcoming everyone in. She looks at everyone's faces curiously as they pass her. When it's our turn to walk in, she stops us.

"Interesting that so many kids have those dots on their faces today," she says.

"They're freckles," Charlie corrects her.

"And they're only ten cents each, if you want some," I say.

"Half the proceeds go to the food bank," adds Amina.

"I assume this is your new business?" Principal Webb asks me. She's about to ask another question, when I assure her that we won't conduct any business dealings on school property.

The second bell rings.

"Gotta go!" I tell her. Then we all run to our classroom.

I take my seat right beside Morten's terrarium. He likes me more than anyone in the class because I write letters to him on the days we have journal writing. I'm also teaching him how to say hello. I place

my palm on the side of his tank and wait
for him. Once he realizes I'm here, he jolts
over and puts his foot on the other side
of the glass like a high five. I toss a dried
cricket into his dish as a reward.

"Morning, Morten!" I say to him.

"*Sabah al-khair!*" Ms. Gelson says to the
class. "Friends, that's how you say 'good
morning' in Arabic!"

"*Sabah al-khair!*" we all reply.

"Everyone, join me on the carpet for show-and-tell this morning," says Ms. Gelson.

We head to the carpet, where Ms. Gelson is waiting. Just as we all sit down, the speaker in the class buzzes, and we hear Principal Webb clear her throat to prepare for her announcement.

"Will the kindergarten class please make their way to the gymnasium to have their school pictures taken," says Principal Webb over the PA system. I wonder how many kids in Mister's class have our freckles.

Fifteen minutes later, we're interrupted by another announcement that crackles over the PA system. "Will Ms. Gelson's class please report to the gymnasium."

It's way too soon for it to be our turn for pictures. There's no way the kindergartners, first graders and second graders have all had their pictures taken already. I don't let myself think it has anything to do with the freckles. It just can't. Can it?

# CHAPTER 12
# Lights, Camera ...

"There they are!" Principal Webb greets us when we enter the gymnasium. It's set up the same as every year for picture day: a chair in front of the camera, a blue backdrop and big lights all around.

Principal Webb has a very fake and somewhat frozen smile plastered to her face. She motions for me, Charlie, Ruby and Ms. Gelson to join her as the photographer paces frantically around the gym. As we make our way over, the rest of my class stands along the back wall with Mister's kindergarten class. The Emmas watch with interest and whisper to one another.

"Wednesday, Charlie, Ruby," says Principal Webb, "this is Wayne, our photographer."

I recognize Wayne. He's been the school photographer since cameras were invented and is super old-fashioned. We never get fun digital backdrops, like a jungle or the solar system.

"Hello," we say together.

"Mister kindly let us know about your freckle business and that you kept a tally of all your customers from yesterday," explains Principal Webb.

I look over at Mister, and he mouths, "Sorry."

"How many children in this school have these spots on their faces?" Wayne demands.

"Freckles," I correct him.

"Spots, dots, freckles!" cries Wayne. "Whatever they are, they've ruined picture day!"

I can tell this makes Charlie upset, but still he manages to say, "We had two hundred and fourteen clients, but some of them were adults."

"More than two hundred?!" says Wayne. He looks like he's going to faint.

The Emmas gulp back their laughter.

"What Wayne is trying to say," Principal Webb says calmly, "is that he is concerned that parents might not want a copy of the photos because of the, er, freckles."

"Our freckles make people feel good about themselves, and that should make for better photos!" I say.

"You should be thanking us!" adds Ruby.

"Thanking you?!" shrieks Wayne. His loud voice has made a kindergartner start to cry. "My reputation is on the line!"

"This is not a big deal," says Ms. Gelson, trying to calm everyone down. "Clearly everyone's parents have already seen the freckles, and Wednesday is right, they are making everyone smile!"

But Ms. Gelson must have forgotten that crying is contagious when you're in kindergarten, because now most of Mister's class is in tears. And that *definitely* isn't good for picture day.

"I will not work under these conditions!"
Wayne screams. He quickly packs up and
storms out of the gym.

Principal Webb has a look on her face I don't recognize. She's not angry. She's not annoyed. I think she's worried.

"Can't we just get another photographer?" asks Charlie.

"Not on such short notice," says Principal Webb, "and we've already paid Wayne a big deposit, so I'm afraid it's not in the budget this year."

I'm worried that this looks like it's all my fault, but telling on the Emmas for planting their permanent markers won't help fix anything at this point.

"I have an idea!" says Ruby. "I just need to make a phone call."

Principal Webb hands Ruby her cell phone without asking any questions, which must mean she's desperate for help.

"Don't worry, Wednesday," says Ruby. "I've got this."

# CHAPTER 13
## Action!

"Raj!" Ruby calls out the gymnasium door twenty minutes later. "Over here!"

"I brought backup," says Raj. Behind him is his whole cosmetology class. They start setting up stations at the far end of the gym while Raj puts his fancy camera on a tripod.

"Thank you so much for coming," says Ms. Gelson, blushing. "I loved your five-minute-face tutorial last week."

"Thank you, gorgeous!" says Raj. "And what grade are you in?"

"She's my teacher, Raj," says Ruby, rolling her eyes. "That's Ms. Gelson."

Raj winks at us. Then he turns his attention to Ruby. "Come here a second, Rubes. I need to see if this works." Raj pours some liquid from a little bottle onto a cotton ball and wipes Ruby's cheek. Her freckles disappear.

"Ta-da!" he exclaims. "Everything's gone!"

"But I thought you liked your freckles, Ruby," says Charlie.

"Don't worry," Raj assures him. "We can always add them back for anyone who wants them — in a less permanent way." He pulls out a small tube and twists off the cap. He uses the pointy wand to place freckles all over Ruby's face.

Raj turns to all the kids in the gym. "Listen up, beautiful people! Today you get to decide on your look for picture day. One of our talented artists will clean up that permanent marker, and then if you still want freckles like Charlie over here, we can give you some."

"And they're washable?" Principal
Webb confirms.

"They'll come right off with soap," Raj
tells her.

"How can we repay you?" Principal
Webb asks. "We don't have anything left
in the budget."

I remember what my mom said yesterday about artists being paid fairly and call my friends together into a huddle. "What do you think about giving our Frecktacular money to Raj and his friends for all their work?" I ask everyone.

"I think that's a good idea," says Charlie.

"Me, too," Mister agrees.

"I'm in," Ruby adds.

I turn to Raj and Principal Webb to tell them our plan.

Now it's Raj's turn for a huddle. He talks to his classmates and then tells us, "We accept the payment so long as it's donated to the food bank."

We all nod.

"It's a deal," I say, and we shake on it.

Everyone runs as fast as they can to line up in rows in front of the artists. And then one by one, each student has their picture taken by Raj. When we're all done, Principal Webb starts calling down the other classes to have their pictures taken.

Any other time, I might feel like Frecktacular was a bust after all that happened today. But even though it didn't work out as I thought, and I didn't make any money, I realize that I can't do any of this without Ruby. And now I don't have to ever again.

# CHAPTER 14
# Nothing More to Tell

Ms. Gelson really is the best teacher in the world. She says we can stay in the gym while all the classes get freckled, and we get to miss math and spelling. In all the flurry, I sneak back to our classroom to get the Emmas' pouch with all their permanent markers inside. I walk over to where the Emmas are standing in the corner.

"I believe this is yours," I say to Emma M., holding the pouch out in front of me between two fingers like it's a bag of toxic waste.

"You can't prove it," she sneers at me. "Everyone loves hearts."

"I'm not going to tell on you, if that's what you're thinking," I say to her. The other Emmas look confused. They love to tell on people.

"You're not?" asks Emma M. She takes the pouch from me.

"There's no point —" I start.

"And there's nothing to tell," Emma M. replies. "But fine, that's good, I guess."

"Good luck with your mole business," I say as I walk away.

When the whole school has finally finished, Raj applies freckles to his own face without even looking in a mirror. When he's done, he takes out his phone to snap a selfie with Ruby. The Emmas scramble to Ruby's side, hoping to get in the picture. They're a second too late but take the chance to start gushing about how good she looks with freckles and how much they've always wanted them. I can see what Ruby was talking about earlier. I can also see her trying to squirm away from them.

"I think it's so cool how you make people beautiful," says Emma M. to Raj. The other Emmas nod their heads enthusiastically.

"The people I work with are already beautiful." Raj smiles. "I just help them celebrate it."

"Ruby is so lucky to have you for her brother," says Emma N.

"And I'm lucky to have her. Family is the most important thing in the world," Raj replies.

"When you post that picture you just took, you'll be the most famous family ever," says Emma M.

"On that note — Wednesday, Mister, Charlie, you should get in here, too," Raj says with a wink. "After all, friends are the family you choose."

The Emmas retreat, speechless for the first time.

Raj takes another picture, this time of the five of us. He whispers he's not going to post it and instead texts it to our moms. Ruby's mom replies immediately with a heart-eyed emoji, and then Charlie's mom sends, "Beautiful!" My stomach clenches when my mom doesn't reply right away.

A moment later, my mom video-calls Raj. Her huge smile fills the screen. I look behind her, and she's not in her studio, she's not even in our house. She's at the taco place!

"My hands are covered in paint, so I couldn't text," she tells us. "You all look amazing, but that's not why I'm calling! I saw you're with Wednesday, and I wanted to tell her the good news right away. The taco place agreed to my fee!"

I feel a huge sense of relief.

Mom asks Raj if he can watch me and Mister after school, since she won't be home until dinnertime.

"Coolio!" says Raj.

"Can you bring home tacos for dinner?"
I ask Mom.

"I'll see what I can do." Right before she ends the call, she says, "I don't know about you, Wednesday, but I'm starting to get kind of sick of pizza."

# THE END

# EPILOGUE*

Dear Morten,

Class picture day was a huge hit. Everyone
in the entire school, even all the teachers
and staff, got freckled. In the end, we
raised even more money for the food
bank, because the grown-ups paid for
their freckles. Our librarian, Ms. Eleanor,
set the record with 150 freckles! You
haven't met Ms. Eleanor yet because she's
afraid of reptiles. Charlie said that's called
herpetophobia, which sounds like this:
*her-pet-o-phobia.*

*A fancy word for the REAL end

One more thing! We decided to do a freckle fundraiser every year for picture day. Since we got to choose the charity this time around, next year another class will get a turn. I don't know what class I'll be in next year, but I hope it's still Ms. Gelson's class for fourth grade. That way we can still hang out every day. Plus, who else is going to high-five me every morning?

Your friend,
Wednesday

# Acknowledgments*

Wednesday Wilson was inspired by, and written with, my two boys, Dario and Oakland. They may be big kids now, but when we started this project years ago, it was because as children of mixed race, they weren't seeing themselves represented in books. I feel an immense privilege to have them lend their voices to the manuscripts to provide authenticity where I, a white woman, would fall short. They also fill me in on what's cool, and what's way too cringe to write.

*A fancy word for saying thank you

My editor, Katie Scott at Kids Can Press, deserves as much praise as anyone for the success of this series. She has a true eagle eye and sees Wednesday as a three-dimensional person living right down the road. Katie is an advocate for each character in the book. She poses hard questions about stereotypes, representation and language, and has an immense amount of respect for the reader. Katie is a gift from the literary goddesses. I continue to learn from her daily.

A humongous thank-you to Morgan Goble, illustrator extraordinaire, whose immeasurable talent is what makes these books spring to life. My kids will forever be reflected in the pages, something we only dreamed possible when we started writing together.

Thank you to my agent, Claire Anderson-Wheeler at Regal Hoffmann, for believing in both me and Wednesday right away. To my dad for reading every word I write, to my partner for letting me read aloud when I think I'm on a roll and to my best friend, Carina, for being my cheerleader. Finally, there are so many moving parts behind the scenes in a series like Wednesday Wilson, and the team at Kids Can Press is second to none. It takes far more than an author to make a book, and I hope they all share in this achievement alongside me.

**Bree Galbraith** is a writer and graphic designer who lives with her family in Vancouver, British Columbia. Her critically acclaimed books include the Wednesday Wilson series, *Nye, Sand and Stones, Usha and the Stolen Sun* and *Milo and Georgie.* Bree holds a Masters in Creative Writing from the University of British Columbia. Visit breegalbraith.com to learn more.

Morgan Goble has been drawing since she could first hold a crayon. A graduate of the Bachelor of Illustration program at Sheridan College, Morgan is the illustrator of *Wednesday Wilson Gets Down to Business* and *Wednesday Wilson Fixes All Your Problems*. She lives with her husband and their cat, Noni, in London, Ontario. To learn more about Morgan, visit morgangoble.ca.

# LOOKING FOR MORE OF THE INDOMITABLE*
# WEDNESDAY WILSON?

"Wednesday is funny and charming and sure to win over readers, especially fans of Ramona Quimby, Marty McGuire and Clementine."
— *School Library Journal*

"A series opener for young fans of Shark Tank and anyone who enjoys bringing ideas to life."
— *Kirkus Reviews*

"This second outing for Wednesday and company is a welcome addition to any early chapter book collection."
— *School Library Journal*

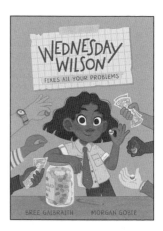

*A fancy word for impossible to defeat